There's a Dragon
IN YOUR BOOK

Written by TOM FLETCHER

Illustrated by GREG ABBOTT

Random House 🏠 New York

For Buzz and Buddy —T.F.

For Susanne —G.A.

Copyright © 2018 by Tom Fletcher
Illustrated by Greg Abbott

All rights reserved. Published in the United States
by Random House Children's Books, a division of Penguin Random House LLC, New York.
Published by Puffin Books, an imprint of Penguin Random House Children's Books, U.K.,
a division of Penguin Random House U.K., London, in 2018.

Random House and the colophon are registered trademarks of Penguin Random House LLC.

Visit us on the Web! rhcbooks.com

Educators and librarians, for a variety of teaching tools, visit us at RHTeachersLibrarians.com

Library of Congress Cataloging-in-Publication Data is available upon request.

ISBN 978-1-5247-6638-2 (trade) — ISBN 978-1-5247-6639-9 (ebook)

MANUFACTURED IN CHINA

10 9 8 7 6 5 4 3 2 1

First American Edition

OH, LOOK!
There's an egg in your book!

It looks ready to hatch.
Whatever you do, don't turn the page. . . .

I can't believe you did that!

The egg hatched, and now there's a
dragon in your book!

Don't be scared—it's a baby dragon!

Go ahead and **tickle** her little nose....

Oops!

The dragon accidentally sneezed
a fire in your book.

We need to
put it out quickly.

Help Dragon **blow** out the flame,
and turn the page.

OH NO,

your dragon didn't blow out the fire.

She blew MORE fire!

Carefully cover the flames
by turning the page, and tamp it down—
that should put them out!

It didn't work . . .
they're getting bigger!

Don't get
too close!

If only we could think of a way
to put out this fire. . . .

THAT'S IT!

Let's use your *imagination*

to put out the fire!

IMAGINE

a great big water balloon
right in the middle of the next page.

Make sure it's full and ready to pop. . . .

PERFECT!

Now use your finger
to **PoP** the balloon,
and get ready for the . . .

Hooray! You put out the fire!

Give the dragon a

HIGH FIVE!

You have a great imagination—and Dragon
must be a little hungry now. . . .

Why don't you use your imagination again
and think up a **yummy treat** for her.

How about a triple scoop of yummy,
ice-cold
chocolate and strawberry . . .

Wow, that looks delicious!

Yum!

Well, Dragon must be tired
after all that adventure.
I think it's time for her to fly home.

She's probably very full.
She's going to need some help taking off.

Flap the book up and down like giant dragon wings. . . .

Almost there—
keep flapping!

There she goes!

Goodbye, Dragon!

Wave goodbye and turn the—

Hang on a second.
What's this?

Oh, look!
More eggs!

Whatever you do,
don't turn
the page. . . .

UH-OH!

I think it's time to close the book.
Carefully . . .